The
Tiara
Club

at Emerald
Castle

For Princess Millie
of Hippy Hill xxx
VF
With very special thanks to JD

www.tiaraclub.co.uk

ORCHARD BOOKS
338 Euston Road, London NW1 3BH
Orchard Books Australia
Level 17/207 Kent St, Sydney, NSW 2000

A Paperback Original
First published in 2008 by Orchard Books
Text © Vivian French 2008
Cover illustration © Sarah Gibb 2008
Inside illustrations © Orchard Books 2008

A CIP catalogue record for this book is available
from the British Library.

ISBN 978 1 84616 872 7

3 5 7 9 10 8 6 4 2

Printed in Great Britain
The paper and board used in this paperback are natural recyclable
products made from wood grown in sustainable forests. The
manufacturing processes conform to the environmental
regulations of the country of origin.

Orchard Books is a division of Hachette Children's Books,
an Hachette Livre UK company.
www.orchardbooks.co.uk

The Tiara Club

at Emerald Castle

Princess Millie

and the Magical Mermaid

By Vivian French

ORCHARD BOOKS

The Royal Palace Academy
for the Preparation of Perfect Princesses

(Known to our students as *"The Princess Academy"*)

OUR SCHOOL MOTTO:
*A Perfect Princess always thinks of others
before herself, and is kind, caring and truthful.*

Emerald Castle offers a complete education for
Tiara Club princesses while taking full advantage of
our seaside situation. The curriculum includes:

*A visit to Emerald Sea
World Aquarium and
Education Pool*

*Swimming lessons
(safely supervised at
all times)*

A visit to Seabird Island

Whale watching

Our headteacher, Queen Gwendoline, is present at all
times, and students are well looked after by the school
Fairy Godmother, Fairy Angora.

Our resident staff and visiting experts include:

*QUEEN MOLLY
(Sports and games)*

*KING JONATHAN
(Captain of the Royal Yacht)*

*LORD HENRY
(Natural History)*

*QUEEN MOTHER MATILDA
(Etiquette, Posture and
Flower Arranging)*

We award tiara points to encourage our Tiara Club princesses towards the next level. All princesses who win enough points at Emerald Castle will be presented with their Emerald Sashes and attend a celebration ball.

Emerald Sash Tiara Club princesses are invited to return to Diamond Turrets, our superb residence for Perfect Princesses, where they may continue their education at a higher level.

PLEASE NOTE:
Princesses are expected to arrive at the Academy with a *minimum* of:

TWENTY BALLGOWNS
(with all necessary hoops, petticoats, etc)

TWELVE DAY DRESSES

SEVEN GOWNS
suitable for garden parties, and other special day occasions

TWELVE TIARAS

DANCING SHOES
five pairs

VELVET SLIPPERS
three pairs

RIDING BOOTS
two pairs

Swimming costumes, playsuits, parasols, sun hats and other essential outdoor accessories as required

Good day, pretty princess! Greetings
from thy faithful friend, Princess Millie!
Eeeek - wouldn't it be SUCH hard work if
we had to talk like that all the time?
It's much nicer to be able to say,
"Hi! How are you?"
Isn't it so lovely here at Emerald Castle?
Amelia, Leah, Ruby, Rachel, Zoe and I just
ADORE being by the sea. We lie in bed
in Daffodil Room and listen to the
waves...and wonder what the
horrible twins will do next!

Chapter One

I think art lessons are my most favourite, especially when we get to go outside. I always go into a sort of dream, and when Queen Molly took us to a rocky beach to paint a sea scene for our school art competition I was SO happy. There were heaps of seaweedy rocks scattered everywhere, just as if a giant had flung handfuls of huge boulders onto the sandy shore, and I was just wondering if I'd drawn them properly when—

"Princess Millie! What a LOVELY picture!"

Queen Molly was standing RIGHT behind me, and I nearly jumped out of my skin. My paint box went flying one way, and my water jar went the other – ALL over Diamonde. She let out a massive screech, and leapt to her feet.

"You did that on purpose, Millie!" Her eyes were positively flashing as she glared at me. "I know you did!"

"I'm really sorry," I apologised, and I searched in my bag for a clean hankie. "Here – use this."

Diamonde ignored me, and turned to Queen Molly. "Can I go back to Emerald Castle? Millie's absolutely RUINED my dress! Mummy'll be FURIOUS – it's the very best satin, you know."

"Rubbish, Diamonde." Queen Molly gave one of her loud cheery laughs. "It's only a drop of water. If you sit over there in the sunshine you'll dry out in no time at all."

Diamonde stuck out her lower lip, but she didn't argue. She picked up her drawing book and paints and stomped off towards an especially large rock, and after a moment or two Gruella went after her.

"I really am sorry, Your Majesty," I said as I picked up my brushes and paints. "Will her dress be OK, do you think?"

Queen Molly made a kind of snorting noise. "Any princess who wears a satin dress for an art lesson is asking for trouble," she said. "Don't give it another thought. Just get on with your beautiful picture!"

Of course that made me glow with pleasure, but I still felt guilty. Diamonde's dress did look dreadful, and I couldn't help thinking Queen Molly might have been just a little bit more sympathetic. Usually Fairy Angora, who's our school assistant fairy godmother, takes us for art lessons, but she was back at

Emerald Castle getting the exhibition ready.

As I went on painting I kept glancing over to where Diamonde and Gruella were sitting all by themselves. They seemed to be busy with their pictures, though, and after a while I forgot about them.

I finished my painting, and started to draw a seagull, but it was SO difficult – I kept having to rub it out and start again. Ruby tried to help, but her seagull looked like a mouse with wings, and it made Amelia and Leah giggle.

"Ask Queen Molly," Rachel suggested, and Zoe nodded. I put my hand up, and Queen Molly came striding over.

"Please," I said, "can you help me with my seagull?"

Queen Molly put her hands on her hips, and peered at my drawing. "I don't think I can, Millie. Maybe you'd better wait until you can ask Fairy Angora. You've done very well, though, you and all of Daffodil Room. I'm sure your pictures will win a prize in the competition!" She gave us one of her beaming smiles. "Now, why don't you go and have a look in the rock pools while everyone else finishes their paintings? But be careful not to go too far, and keep well away from the caves under the rocks. The tide comes in very quickly here, and I don't want any of you caught by the sea!"

Chapter Two

As we hurried over the sand
I thought that maybe I could
tell Diamonde how sorry I was
about her dress, but as soon as the
twins saw us coming they got up.

"Come along now, Gruella!"
Diamonde tidied her painting into
her bag, and took her sister's arm.
"Here come the daft Daffodillies.

Let's go and find a nice quiet place, before they ruin YOUR dress as well!" And she marched Gruella away in between the rocky boulders.

"Oh well," Zoe said. "If they

want to be like that I suppose it's up to them."

"They'll get over it." Leah hopped onto a large stone. "Hey! I'm the king of the castle!"

Amelia laughed, and gave her a push. "Not now you're not. Anyway, shouldn't that be queen of the castle?"

Rachel grinned at us. "'Every Perfect Princess hopes to be a Perfect Queen one day,'" she quoted, and she swept a wonderful curtsey before swinging herself onto the first of a long line of rocks that stretched across the sand towards the waves.

"Come and see!" she called down. "There's a wonderful view, and LOADS of rock pools!"

We hurried after her, but none of us are as good at climbing as Rachel, and by the time we caught up with her she was already peering into a pool. "Look!" she said. "There's a fabulous pink sea anemone!"

We all crouched down, and she was right. It was very lovely, but as we stared into the water I saw something else. "What's that?" I asked, and I dipped my hand into the clear water, and pulled out the prettiest string of pale green pearls.

"Ooooh!" My friends gazed at it, their eyes wide.

"It's just BEAUTIFUL!" Ruby whispered. "The pearls look like drops of sea water! Who could it belong to?"

I shook my head. "Who knows? Maybe a sea princess..."

Zoe gave a loud gasp. "Or a mermaid! Can you imagine... wouldn't it be SO amazing if we really truly saw a mermaid?"

We looked at each other, hardly daring to breathe. And then Diamonde's voice sneered from down on the sand below, "A MERMAID? Goodness! What silly babies you are. Did you hear that, Gruella?"

Gruella sniggered. "WE know there aren't any such things, don't we?"

"We certainly do." I couldn't see Diamonde, but I absolutely knew her nose was in the air. "And it seems those horrid Daffodillies are following us. Let's go and see what's in those caves by the water's edge. You never know – we might find a mermaid of our very own!" Diamonde laughed loudly at her own joke, and a moment later we saw the twins come out from the shadow of our rocks and make their way towards the sea.

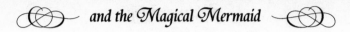

"Didn't Queen Molly say we weren't to go near the caves?" I asked Amelia. She nodded, and I stood up.

"Diamonde! Gruella!" I shouted. "Queen Molly said not to go to the caves! It isn't safe!"

I know the twins heard me, because Diamonde shrugged her shoulders, and Gruella half looked behind her...but they just went on walking.

Leah frowned. "Should we go after them?"

"Maybe." Rachel squinted into the sunshine. "I'm sure the tide's coming in...isn't the sea much nearer than when we started painting?"

"They'll be OK as long as they don't do anything stupid," Zoe said, and then she paused. "But suppose they go into a cave, and get trapped?"

"I think we should follow them," I said firmly. "If we creep along the rocks we can keep an eye on the twins, and they won't know. Do we all agree?"

And all of Daffodil Room put up their hands.

Chapter Three

It was fun tiptoeing along the rocks. There were lots more pools, and we stopped to look in each one, but we didn't find anything else exciting. I was still holding the necklace we'd found, and it was cool and smooth in my hand – until I suddenly felt a faint tingling in my fingers.

I looked down, and the pearls were positively glowing.

"Wow," I said, and I showed Amelia. "Do you think it could be magic?"

"It must be. REALLY magic." Amelia sounded awestruck. She took the necklace from me, but immediately the pearls looked ordinary. "Oh! It's gone all dull!"

Amelia looked so sad that Leah came to see what we were doing, and we explained about the pearls changing colour. "Maybe," Leah said slowly, "it's got something to do with which way you're facing." She picked up the necklace, and moved towards the sea – and at once the pearls shone even brighter than before. Leah nodded. "I think it knows where it belongs. I think it'll get brighter and brighter the nearer we get."

Zoe, Ruby and Rachel came crowding round us, and we experimented with walking first one way, and then another...and

Leah was right. The pearls only shone when we went in one particular direction.

"Should we go the way it wants us to go?" I asked.

My friends nodded. "Perhaps we really will see a mermaid," Zoe said hopefully. "After all, it MUST belong to someone very magical."

"That would be amazing," I agreed, and we set off again along the rocks. This time we didn't stop to look in any pools, and in no time we were balancing on the last rock of all. Immediately beneath it was a tiny sandy shore, but the waves were rushing in on either side of us, and we could tell that when the tide was high the rock we stood on would be an island.

"What do we do now?" Rachel asked. "We can't go any further out – not without swimming!"

I looked at the necklace, and it was shining so very brightly I couldn't believe I'd ever thought the pearls were pale green. They were as brilliant as emeralds – and my fingers were tingling unbearably. Before I knew what I was doing I swung my arm, and threw the necklace into the water.

"What are you DOING—?" Zoe began, and then she stopped, and we stared...and stared.

A small white arm had come out of the waves, and caught the necklace – and a second later a little mermaid rose out of the sea.

She looked SO happy as she waved to us – and then she was gone.

We were all completely silent for what seemed like ages, until Amelia whispered, "Did you see what I saw? A real live mermaid?"

And that was when we heard the scream...

"HELP! HELP! WE'RE GOING TO DROWN!"

Chapter Four

It was Diamonde's voice, and it sounded very near...but we couldn't see her or Gruella. I lay down on the rock edge and wriggled forward, and still I couldn't see anything. Ruby grabbed one of my legs, and Leah the other, and I moved as far forward as I dared – and then

I saw the twins. They were
standing on a tiny strip of sand
immediately below me, and their
shoes were already wet...and all
around them were waves.

"Diamonde!" I yelled. "Gruella!
Can you hear me?"

Gruella twisted round, and stared up at me, her face very pale. "Millie! I'm so scared! We were in the cave under the rock, and we didn't see the sea coming up!"

"You've got to get us out of here!" Diamonde was as pale as Gruella. "We can't climb the rock – it's much too steep... PLEASE help us!"

As Diamonde spoke a little wave broke right over Gruella's feet, and she gave a scream, and clutched Diamonde. "We're going to drown! Oh, I know we're going to drown!"

Princess Millie

"No you're not!" I hoped
I sounded as if I meant what I was
saying. "We'll save you – just
hang on another minute or two!"

I scrabbled backwards, and as
I sat up I saw Leah and Rachel
hurrying back the way we'd come.

"They've gone to get Queen
Molly," Zoe told me. "Oh – don't
you WISH Fairy G or Fairy
Angora was here? They'd be able
to magic the twins to safety."

I totally agreed with Zoe, but it
wasn't any good wishing. Every
second the water was getting
higher, and I knew we had to do
something – we couldn't wait.

"I know!" Ruby jumped up, and looked wildly around. "Millie, Zoe – have you got anything we can tie into a rope?"

Zoe began to take off her sash, but I was looking out to sea. Had I imagined it, or had I really seen a golden-haired girl watching us as she slipped in and out of the waves? I waved my arms like windmills, and shouted as loudly as I could, "Little mermaid! Little mermaid! Please – we need your help!"

For a moment that felt like forever nothing happened – and then I saw her. She came swimming round to the other side of our rock, where the water was deeper, and looked up at me with a frown.

"You shouldn't call me 'little mermaid'," she pouted. "I'm a princess, and you should call me 'Your Highness'."

"Oh – I'm so very sorry, Your Highness," I apologised, and I did my best to curtsey. "But please – we really REALLY need your help! Our friends are caught by the tide!"

The mermaid swam a little way away so she could peek round the rock at the twins. She looked even crosser when she came back. "I don't want to help them," she said. "I heard them talking in the cave.

They're silly. They said they didn't believe in mermaids."

"Oh – I'm sure they do really!" I tried desperately to think of some way of persuading her to help us. "Please—"

Amelia came to stand beside me. "Dear Sea Princess," she said, "Millie found your necklace for you – couldn't you help us just this once?"

The little mermaid ignored Amelia, and swam closer. "Why do you wear sparkly crowns on your heads?"

"They're called tiaras," I said, "and we wear them because we're princesses."

The mermaid's eyes opened very wide. "Are those silly girls princesses too?"

I nodded. "Oh – PLEASE can you help them? It would be such

a wonderfully kind and princessy thing to do—"

But as I looked hopefully at the little mermaid there was a sudden swirl in the water, and she was gone.

Chapter Five

I felt absolutely terrible as I gazed at the spot where the mermaid had disappeared. What would happen to Diamonde and Gruella now? I turned to see what Zoe and Ruby were doing.

"It's hopeless," Ruby said, and there were tears in her eyes. "You know how in stories they tear strips off their dresses and make them into ropes? Well, I can't tear my dress at all – the material's MUCH too..."

She stopped without finishing her sentence, and I saw she was staring over my shoulder. I swung round, and my mouth dropped open in amazement.

An empty rowing boat was positively flying over the waves towards us. It was headed straight for the bottom of the rock we were standing on, and I heard Diamonde and Gruella shriek with excitement as they saw it too.

With a final surge the boat
grounded itself on the tiny sandy
strip where the twins were already
up to their ankles in water.

And that was when I saw the little mermaid again. She was behind the boat, hidden away from Diamonde and Gruella. I realised she must have been pushing it...and she wasn't on her own. There were three other little mermaids with her, and when they caught my eye they waved cheerfully before all four disappeared with a flip! flip! of their scaly green tails.

"Thank you! Thank you so much, Your Highness!" I yelled. "You're a Perfect Princess..." And I'm ALMOST sure I saw a little white hand give me a wave.

From down below Diamonde's voice called up, "Millie! MILLIE! Here's a boat!" But then Gruella wailed, "But we can't row! Now we'll be washed out to sea and never see Mummy again!"

I lay back down on the top of the rock, and peered over at them.

They had climbed into the boat, but were clinging to each other at one end, and I could see that it wouldn't be very long before they floated away. I swallowed hard as I made my decision.

"'A Perfect Princess always does what she can to help those in distress!'" I told myself, and I turned round so my legs were hanging over the edge of the rock. It felt as if it was a sheer drop to the water beneath, but my feet found a couple of tiny crevices and I half slid, half climbed as far as I could. Amelia, Ruby and Zoe watched anxiously from above, and my heart began to pound as I tried to find another foothold. My hands were getting trembly, and I wasn't sure how long I could hold on – and then there was a sudden scream from Gruella, a shout from Diamonde, and a MASSIVE wave came roaring up to the rock and swept me into the

water. It was SO cold – but before I had time to even think of swimming, the weirdest thing happened. Lots of little hands grabbed me, and a moment later I was in the boat, rubbing water out of my eyes and blinking up at Diamonde and Gruella.

"What happened?" I gasped.

"You fell off the rock," Diamonde said. She was hanging on to the side of the boat, and shaking.

Gruella nodded. "We saw you fall in the sea...but somehow the very next minute you were in the boat."

"The mermaids caught me," I explained as I picked up the oars.

The twins looked at each other, and then at me. "MERMAIDS?"

"That's right," I said, and I leant forward. "You DO believe in mermaids, don't you?"

A sudden shower of shining water drops flew in the air, and Diamonde squealed...and then saw the way I was looking at her.

"Oh!" she said. "Yes...yes I do."

Gruella nodded her head. "I DEFINITELY believe in them," she said.

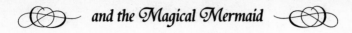
and the Magical Mermaid

And the boat seemed to lift in the water, and it absolutely ZOOMED round the rocks and up to the beach...

And I was just helping Diamonde and Gruella out as Queen Molly came puffing towards us.

Chapter Six

Of course Queen Molly was SHOCKED when she saw Diamonde and Gruella's wet shoes, and my soaking clothes, and before we could say a word she was hurrying us up to Emerald Castle to get changed. She asked us questions all the way, but she didn't really listen to the answers.

By the time we reached the school doors she'd decided I'd brought the boat round to save Diamonde and Gruella, and although I tried to tell her about the little mermaid she just laughed.

"Really, Millie!" she said. "Emerald Castle has been here for years and years, and I've never ever seen a mermaid! Now, run along and get dry. Don't forget Fairy Angora is judging your pictures this evening before we have our celebration supper!"

"OH!" I clutched my head. "My painting! I left it at the beach!"

Queen Molly shook her head. "Rachel and Leah collected up all your things. Your picture is definitely going in the exhibition!"

It was. And guess what – I won a prize! But the most AMAZING thing was that when I looked at my picture, there was something extra in it. In the distance, sitting on a rock, was the tiny figure of a mermaid...

"I didn't paint that," I told Fairy

Angora. "I really didn't!"

Fairy Angora smiled at me. "Mermaids are strange things, Millie. Some people see them, and some people don't – but they always remember a good deed."

She smiled again, and went to talk to Queen Molly – and Ruby came dashing towards me.

"Millie! THERE you are!

Hurry up – it's time for the celebration supper and there are TWENTY different kinds of jelly and the MOST enormous cake..."

The celebration supper was fabulous, and I enjoyed every single

minute – but at the back of my mind I couldn't help wondering about the little mermaid.

When we were snuggling down under our covers in Daffodil Room that night I asked Amelia, "We did REALLY see a mermaid, didn't we?"

Amelia yawned. "We certainly did – she was real!"

Rachel laughed. "Leah and I did too! Your painting blew into the sea, and a dear little mermaid swam up to us, and handed it back. But it was SO weird – no one else noticed her at all!"

"I think she decided she was your friend, Millie," Ruby said from halfway under her pillow. "Friends look after each other..."

That's the lovely thing about friends...

And I'm so very VERY glad you're my friend too!

Don't miss  website at:

www.tiaraclub.co.uk

Keep up to date with the latest
Tiara Club books and meet all
your favourite princesses!

There is SO much to see and do,
including games and activities. You can
even become an exclusive member of the
Tiara Club Princess Academy.

PLUS, there's an exciting
Emerald Castle competition
with a truly AMAZING prize!

Be a Perfect Princess – check it out today!

What happens next?
Find out in

Princess Rachel

and the Dancing Dolphin

Hello, best friend! This is me, Rachel.
Do you love parties and balls as much as
I do? When Amelia, Leah, Ruby, Millie,
Zoe and I first heard there was going to be
a Sea Sparkle Ball at our school we talked
about NOTHING ELSE for weeks! Of course
the horrible twins kept telling us they'd have
the prettiest dresses, but that's just typical
of Diamonde and Gruella...

"Daffodil Room! This must be the THIRD time I've spoken to you, and not ONE of you is paying attention! What ARE you thinking of?"

We jumped guiltily, and I did my best to smile apologetically at Lord Henry. "I'm so sorry," I said. "Er...what was the question?"

Lord Henry rolled his eyes, and sighed heavily. "I was asking if you wanted to travel together when we go to Seabird Island tomorrow."

Of course there was only one answer to that, and we all said, "Yes, PLEASE!"

"Hmm." Lord Henry gave us a stern look. "Just make sure you're all wide awake when we get there," he said. "I'll be asking questions about all the birds I've told you about today, and I do NOT want to find Daffodil Room coming last! You're a very bright group of girls – don't let me down."

"We won't," Amelia promised, but as we filed out of the classroom she whispered, "Oooops! We won't know any of the answers!"

"I wish I'd been listening," Leah said gloomily. "Lord Henry's so nice. I feel awful now."

"Me too," I said, and I meant it. I'd spent the whole lesson imagining myself swooping round the Sea Sparkle Ball in my very best dress, and I hadn't heard a word...

And then I had an idea.

"Maybe we could look it all up in the library?" I suggested. "If we work really hard we might even come first!"

Leah and Amelia nodded, and Ruby, Millie and Zoe made enthusiastic agreeing noises.

~ *Want to read more?* ~
Princess Rachel and the Dancing Dolphin is out now!

This summer, look out for

Emerald Ball

ISBN: 978 1 84616 881 9

Two stories in one fabulous book!